TALES OF ANCIENT CIVILIZATIONS

RETOLD TIMELESS CLASSICS

Perfection Learning®

Retold by Karen Berg Douglas

Editor: Paula J. Reece
Illustrator: Michael A. Aspengren

For information, contact
Perfection Learning® Corporation
1000 North Second Avenue, P.O. Box 500
Logan, Iowa 51546-0500.
Phone: 800-831-4190 • Fax: 712-644-2392

Paperback ISBN 0-7891-5066-2
Cover Craft® ISBN 0-7807-9034-0
Printed in the U.S.A.

Table of Contents

A Young Prince Named Siegfried

Can a person do something that everyone claims is impossible? What does it take? Does it take magic? Or can a person accomplish the unthinkable by just combining skill and determination?

Once upon a time there lived a young prince named Siegfried.

His father, King Siegmund, was known far and wide throughout Germany for the good deeds he did. And Siegfried's mother, the gentle Sigelind, was loved by everyone because she was so kind to the poor.

The king and queen loved their young son very much. Every year they brought wise men from faraway lands to Germany to teach Siegfried about the world. They wanted him to be ready to rule the kingdom someday.

No other young man could shoot an arrow and hit the target more often. Or run faster. Or ride a horse better than Siegfried could.

What's more, everyone in the kingdom loved young Siegfried.

But the old king wanted something more for his son.

"All work is noble. If Siegfried is going to be successful, he must learn how to earn a living with his hands," he said. "And I know someone who may be able to help him."

A few days later, the king sent his son to live with an old blacksmith named Mimer. He was a wonderful teacher—the best that anyone had ever seen. Some said he had a magic well on his land. And anyone who drank the water from it would become very wise.

That would be nice, thought the king. But he wanted no special favors for his son. Siegfried was to be given a blue blouse, heavy trousers, a leather apron, and wooden shoes for his feet. Just like the other students. His head was to be covered with a cap made from the skin of a wolf.

Siegfried would eat plain, simple food. And at night he would sleep on a bale of hay.

Siegfried did not complain. He liked it there. And he liked to work with his hands. He was a good blacksmith—the best student at the school.

He could make anything quickly and well.

One morning, though, Mimer came to the school with a troubled look on his face. When the students saw him, they knew right away that something was very wrong.

"I have always been told that I am the best blacksmith in the whole, wide world," Mimer began. "But a few days ago I heard that another man is taking my title away from me."

"Why, who is this man who dares to say such a thing?" asked one of the students.

"His name is Amilias, and he is from Burgundyland," Mimer said. "Amilias said he has made a strong suit of armor. He said no sword can dent it. And no spear can scratch it."

The students looked at one another. That couldn't be true!

"So I have been working hard the past few days. I must make a sword that will prove that I am still the best blacksmith in the world. But I can't seem to do it," Mimer said.

"Maybe I am too old. You are all young. Do any of you think you can make such a sword?"

No one said a word.

"I have heard a lot about the strength of that wonderful armor," said Veliant, Mimer's assistant. "I don't think anyone can make a sword sharp enough to scratch it."

Mimer looked around the room. His eyes rested on Siegfried.

"I will do it," said the young prince. "I will make a sword that will be sharp and strong. Just give me some time."

The students began to laugh.

"Wait a minute," said Mimer. "He may be the king's son, but we all know he has a lot of talent. Before we judge him, let's see what he can do."

Siegfried went to his table to begin the task. He worked for seven days and seven nights.

On the eighth day he finished and took the sword to Mimer.

"This seems very sharp," said the master blacksmith. He ran his fingers up and down the edge. "Let's see what it can do."

Mimer threw a thin piece of thread into a pool of water. While it was floating, he hit it with the sword. The thread broke in two.

"Well done!" shouted Mimer. "Never have I seen a sharper sword than this one! Now if you can make it strong, it will serve me well."

So Siegfried took the sword again and broke it into many pieces. For three days he welded it together in a white-hot fire until it was whole again.

When he was finished, he threw a ball of wool into a brook. Mimer held the sword in his hands. When the ball of wool reached the sword, it was cut in two. And not a single thread was out of place!

But Siegfried was still not happy with his work.

He went back to his corner in the blacksmith shop and built a bigger fire. He told everyone to stay away.

Some of the students thought he was performing some sort of magic. Some said later that they had seen a one-eyed man with a long white beard talking to Siegfried!

But all agreed that the young prince worked hard and long.

One morning Siegfried went to Mimer with the shiny sword in his hands.

"I have finally finished," he said proudly. "Let us test it one more time. Then we will know whether it will be sharp and strong enough for you."

Mimer looked long and hard at the sword. It shined as bright as any star he had seen on a dark night. What's more, the young prince had engraved beautiful pictures on its handle.

Young Siegfried lifted the sword high above his head and brought it down upon a thick block of iron.

The block of iron broke into two pieces—and there wasn't a single scratch on the blade!

Then they went to the brook where they

threw a big ball of yarn into the stream. As it began to float along, Mimer placed the beautiful sword into the water. The ball of yarn broke into two pieces!

"Now, at last, I am not afraid to meet Amilias," said Mimer. "If this good sword is what it seems to be, I will still be known as the best blacksmith in Germany!"

A few weeks later the two blacksmiths decided to meet and see which was better—Amilias' armor or Mimer's sword. Nearly everyone in both villages turned out to watch the contest.

Finally Amilias put on his shiny armor. He went to the top of a hill and sat down on a rock to wait for Mimer. That is because he could not stand.

The war coat was hard, heavy, and strong. Some say Amilias looked like a giant sitting there.

Up the hill came Mimer. He was a small old man who had trouble reaching the top.

Amilias was not afraid of an old man holding a piece of metal. This was just a silly game.

Meanwhile, Mimer's friends stood quietly by, saying nothing. When he reached the top of the hill, Amilias stood up, folded his big arms, and smiled.

"Are you ready?" asked Mimer.

"Of course I'm ready," laughed Amilias. "Strike."

Mimer raised the shining sword high above his head and brought it down at the neck of the heavy armor.

Amilias didn't move.

"Are you all right?" asked Mimer.

"Yes, of course," replied Amilias.

"Then stand up," Mimer said.

As soon as he did, Amilias' armor separated from neck to toe. It fell into two pieces and rolled down the hill into the river below.

Amilias sat very still, as though he didn't understand what had just happened.

Mimer, the master, placed the sword into his shield and walked down the hill. There his friends stood and cheered.

Of course, no one but the students knew that Siegfried had made the sword.

But after a while some of the students began whispering about the talented prince. And soon word traveled throughout the kingdom.

But no one ever admitted that Siegfried had made the invincible sword. His students still respected Mimer. And they wanted him to keep his title as best blacksmith in the kingdom. But the citizens of the kingdom continued to look at Siegfried with wonder. And Siegfried became one of the most respected kings ever.

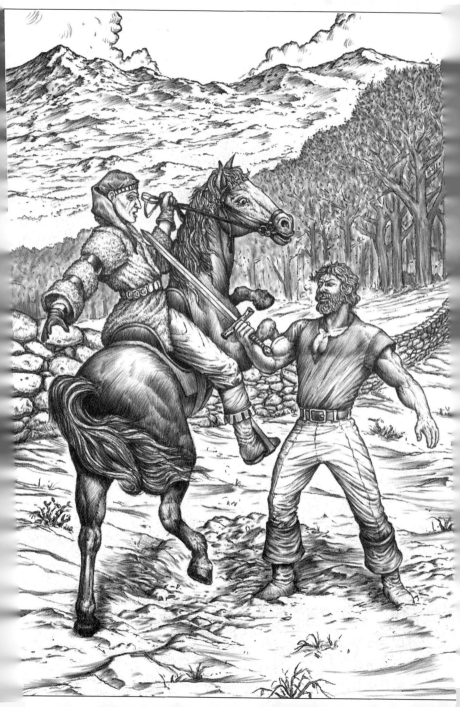

Grettir

Becomes *an* Outlaw

◆ ◆ ◆ ◆

How does it feel to be accused of something you didn't do? What can you do if no one believes you? Do you become the person everyone thinks you are? Or do you remain true to yourself?

$\mathcal{S}$ome say that Grettir was the strongest man who ever lived in the beautiful country of Iceland.

Robbers, giants, and witches stayed out of his way because they were afraid of him.

But Grettir was not happy.

It had become too quiet in the little town where he lived.

One day he heard that some men were traveling north by boat. They were headed across the ocean to Norway. They were looking to find jobs with King Olaf Haraldson.

Grettir decided to go too.

It was late in the year. The days were short, and the nights were cold and long. But Grettir liked the excitement of being on a big ship with so many others.

One evening the sailors tried to reach land. But the waves were too big and rough. So they were forced to dock at an island. There was no shelter there to keep them warm. And they had no way to start a fire. Everyone was afraid they would freeze before morning.

"Look, there are some lights coming from a building over there," said one of the sailors. "Do you think we should try to sail there?"

"I don't know," said another. "The waves still look very big to me."

"But will we be safe here until morning?" asked a third man.

They didn't know what to do.

"Is anyone willing to swim across the dark, cold water to the mainland to try to find help?" asked the first man.

The second man suddenly pointed at Grettir. "Say, you have been called the bravest and strongest of all men in Iceland. Could you do it?" he asked.

Grettir thought a moment.

"Of course, I could do it," he replied proudly. "But how will you reward me for such a dangerous swim?"

"We will reward you well," said the sailor.

"All right then, I will go," said Grettir.

And he took off his heavy coat and jumped into the icy water.

It took Grettir nearly an hour to reach the other side. As he climbed over the rocks and onto the shore, his hair, beard, and clothes froze stiff in the cold and wind.

Grettir began to shake as he walked toward the light that was coming from a big building. He opened the door. Inside he found about one hundred men eating dinner.

"Halooo," began Grettir. "I wonder if you can help me and my shipmates."

The men jumped up from their chairs. They thought Grettir was a sea monster!

They grabbed their big sticks and started toward him.

Grettir was wet and cold. But he was still very strong. He took the sticks out of their hands easily.

"He must be an evil spirit," someone shouted. "Let's burn him!"

Everyone grabbed a burning torch that was being used to light the hall. Within a few minutes one of the torches set fire to a pile of straw.

All of a sudden the whole building was burning!

Grettir grabbed a torch and ran out the door and down to the shore. He leaped into the cold water and began to swim back to his shipmates.

It was not easy.

The waves were high and pulled him this way and that. And all the time, Grettir had to hold the burning torch up so no water would put out the fire.

It took him nearly two hours.

Finally he reached land where his shipmates waited and welcomed him. They built a big fire and went to sleep.

Meanwhile the men on the mainland were upset that Grettir got away.

"I saw him go down to the shore and jump into the sea," said one. "He must have been a monster!"

But the hour was late, and they were very tired. They had put out all the fires in the building. So they decided to lie down and get some sleep.

Sadly, they overlooked some hot ashes that were still burning. In a matter of seconds, the fire climbed the wall and reached the roof. And it came tumbling down on the sleeping men.

The next morning when Grettir and his

shipmates awoke, the sun was shining, and the wind had died down. When they returned to their ship, they saw the gray smoke still coming from the great fire.

"Let's go and see what we can find," said one of the shipmates.

But when they got there, all they found were the burned bones.

"Why did you burn those men?" asked one of the men.

"How could I burn them?" Grettir asked. "There was no fire to be seen when we went to sleep."

But the men were not sure they believed him. And they weren't sure they wanted him aboard.

Grettir and his shipmates went back to the boat and continued north toward Norway. The next time the ship docked, Grettir's shipmates were ready with a plan. When Grettir went ashore, his shipmates sailed away without him.

Wherever they stopped, they told how Grettir had burned some men in the big hall. Days later when Grettir began to sail with another ship traveling northward, he soon found people had turned against him—even King Olaf.

Several weeks passed before the king finally agreed to see Grettir.

"An evil tale has been told against me, dear

king, and I wish to clear myself of it," Grettir said.

"Well, then, tell me your story. And I will listen to you," said King Olaf.

When he finished, Grettir begged the king to tell everyone what had really happened.

"I have listened to you speak, and I believe you are telling the truth," said King Olaf. "But I think you are being followed by evil spirits. The only way to get rid of them is for you to come to the church, a holy place, and put your hand on a hot iron."

"Oh, thank you, thank you, my king," said Grettir.

He was strong. This would be an easy thing for him to do.

A few days later a big crowd gathered outside the church to watch. As Grettir walked toward the door, a small man jumped out of the crowd. He had a big head, wild eyes, and orange hair. He began to point and shout at Grettir.

"Look at this evil sea monster," he shouted as he jumped up and down. "This man burned helpless men for no reason. And soon he will walk away free!"

Grettir became very angry—so angry that he hit the funny-looking little man and knocked him down.

Meanwhile the king was waiting inside. When

he heard the noise, he came to the door and found Grettir looking all around for the little man. But by this time the little man had run away.

"I'm sorry, my son, but after all this it will not be possible to clear your name by using a hot iron," the king said.

Grettir was very sad.

"But, my king, I have come all the way from Iceland to work for you," Grettir said. "I have just had a lot of bad luck. Since you see how strong I am, could you not use another bodyguard?"

"No, my son. It would not work," said King Olaf. "It is true you have more courage and strength than any of my men. But your bad luck will bring trouble to everyone who is with you. And I cannot take a chance on that."

"But how can my name be cleared?" asked Grettir. "I did not burn those men."

"I don't know," said King Olaf. "You have some kind of evil curse on you. And because there is always trouble when you are around, I will have to ask you to leave my kingdom."

Grettir had no friends and no money. He could do nothing. So he decided to start walking to his brother's house several hundred miles away.

He walked during the day and slept under a tree in the forest at night. Even though it got very dark, he was not afraid.

Right around Christmas, Grettir came to the house of a farmer named Einar who was very rich and kind. He was planning a big celebration for the holiday. And he invited Grettir to stay.

But two days after Christmas when all of Einar's Christmas guests had gone home, someone began knocking loudly on the front door.

"Come out! Come out, you old man!" shouted a voice.

"Heaven, help us!" said Einar to Grettir. "It is Snaekol and his mean men. I think they have come to rob me!"

Einar walked to the door and went outside.

Grettir was right behind him.

There sat a dozen men on their horses.

"You must give us all your goods and your house or else fight with me to keep them," Snaekol shouted.

"I cannot fight," Einar said. "I am old and weak. And I have no strength in my arms."

"Well, then, what about that big man who stands beside you?" asked Snaekol.

"I'm not very strong either," said Grettir.

"You both are afraid of me," laughed Snaekol.

He rode his horse close to the two men and took his sword from his shield. Grettir took a quick step forward and grabbed the sword from Snaekol.

Snaekol looked at Grettir in surprise.

"Go, and go quickly, before I harm you. And do not come and bother this old man or anyone else here ever again," Grettir said. He had the sword pointed at Snaekol's chest.

Snaekol jerked on the reins of his horse and turned toward the woods. His men followed close behind.

The next morning Grettir said good-bye to his friend and continued his walk toward his brother's home.

No one heard anything more from Grettir that year. So no one knows if bad luck continued to follow him.

But Grettir's good deed was remembered for many years by Einar and all those who lived around him.

The Empty City

Many years ago, long before there was radio, television, or computers, people entertained themselves by telling stories to one another.

Sometimes they carried their stories from one village to another. Just like the mail carrier does with our letters today.

These stories are called folktales.

Some say they really happened a long time ago. Others say they just couldn't be true. This is one of those stories.

But whether it's true or not is left up to you.

Once upon a time there was a very brave and clever soldier named Chuko. He lived in the great Empire of the Hans in China.

One day it was decided that the Empire would be divided into three parts.

They would be called the Kingdoms of Wei, Wu, and Shu.

Wei was the strongest. Wu was only so-so. And little Shu was very weak compared to the other two kingdoms.

The people of these three kingdoms were very jealous of one another. So every now and then, two of the kingdoms would team up and go to war against the third one.

But most of the time, they were fighting against one another. Trying to see which kingdom was the strongest and the best.

One day the people of the big Kingdom of Wei decided to march on the little Kingdom of Shu.

The Wei folk were sure they would have an easy victory.

What they did not know, though, was that Shu had something much better than a big army.

They had Chuko—the commander in chief of the Shu armies and a truly great general. He also was the premier, the leader of Shu.

And some believed there was no one wiser in any of the three kingdoms than Chuko.

Well, maybe one.

His name was Hua, the great commander of the Wei army. He had already decided to lead his army to the Chieh Ting Pass and capture Chuko and the Shus!

Now no one knew that, of course. Not even the Intelligence Horsemen who roamed the kingdom day and night.

No one—except Chuko.

He knew.

Chuko had a way of knowing things. Some said he was a wizard. Some said Sing, the Star God, had given him six senses instead of five, like most people have.

Others said he used magic.

Maybe it had something to do with all the strange instruments he used to measure the planets and the heavens every day.

Whatever it was, Chuko knew what was happening on the other side of those big mountains in the big Kingdom of Wei.

But there was no time to ask him any questions. The Wei army was getting close to the pass. Chuko called for Zhi, one of his great generals.

"You must go quickly to the Chieh Ting Pass and defend it," said Chuko. And he began drawing a map.

"Pitch your tent here on this spot. Send your men out when the Wei army gets close to you. Once you are there, make a map and send me a copy right away. That way I will know where everyone is.

"Now be off with you—quickly," Chuko said.

Zhi was a great general and a man of great courage. But he had one big fault. He thought no one was as clever as he. So he didn't listen very carefully to everything that Chuko had said to him.

But off they went—General Zhi, Wang, who was second in command, and the Shu army.

By the time they reached the Chieh Ting Pass, Zhi had forgotten everything that Chuko had told him to do.

"No matter," said Zhi. "I have some pretty good ideas of my own."

And after all, his opinion was far more valuable than all of the gold, jade, and jewels in the three kingdoms. Wasn't it?

Wang shook his head. He remembered what Chuko had said to Zhi. But he was only second in command, so he could do nothing.

And what about the map?

Well, Zhi didn't make one. He had forgotten all about it.

Now Wang was an honest soldier who always did what he was told. And he didn't want to get in any trouble. So without telling Zhi, he made a little map himself. Then he called a messenger and told him to take it to Chuko.

Meanwhile, Hua and his army arrived at the Chieh Ting Pass. They cut off the water supply to the Zhi forces, forcing them to move back to Shu. With that victory behind them, they marched on to Hsi Cheng, West City.

Of course, Chuko knew what had happened even before the messenger arrived with the map. Remember, he always knew things before they happened.

He also knew that the Wei Army was on its way to Hsi Cheng.

In a matter of minutes, Chuko divided up the remaining men and sent them off throughout the Shu Kingdom to keep it safe.

Then with only a handful of soldiers, he marched on to Hsi Cheng, West City. Just as they reached the city, an Intelligence Horseman rode up on horseback with some bad news.

"Hua and his 150,000 soldiers are coming this way at full speed," the Intelligence Horseman said.

People began coming out of their houses to see what all the excitement was about.

"Oh, no! Oh, no! What will become of our beautiful city?" they cried. "Is there nothing we can do? They will take our beautiful city away from us!"

The soldiers turned pale. The people shook with fright.

Chuko said nothing. Very calmly he walked to the wall of the city and climbed the steps to the top of the watchtower.

There in the distance, he heard the sound and saw the great cloud of dust. It was being stirred up by the horses of the Wei soldiers.

And the sound was getting closer!

Chuko climbed down from the watchtower and turned to the people.

"Take down all the flags and banners from the buildings, houses, shops, and temples in this city," he began. "Hide them well. Then hide yourselves even better. When the enemy comes, don't make a sound, or show yourself, or go outside the city wall."

The people looked at their hero, nodded their heads, and began to move quietly and quickly.

Then Chuko turned to the 20 Shu soldiers. He ordered them to remove their uniforms and change into ordinary clothes.

"Then I want you to open the four gates of the city," Chuko said.

The soldiers looked at one another in surprise. But they quickly did as they were told. Although they did not understand the order, they had great respect for their leader.

Just as they finished, the Wei Intelligence Horsemen appeared at the gates of Hsi Cheng, West City.

Everything was so quiet. There were no soldiers in sight.

What did this mean?

They turned around and quickly rode back to tell Hua.

"How can that be so?" asked Hua when he heard their report. "You, my chief officer, take some more scouts and check again."

But it was true.

When the Wei scouts arrived, they rode around the walls and looked through the gates. There were no Shu soldiers in Hsi Cheng.

All they saw were about 20 street workers. They were sweeping up leaves in and around the gate to the city.

Then the Wei scouts looked up toward the watchtower. There sat a gray-haired old man. He was dressed in a beautiful robe with flying cranes, wearing a silk *jun-chin* hermit's hat.

And there, on either side of him, were *chin* boys. They were placing a long wooden board in front of the hermit with a chin of seven strings.

Oh, yes! There it was!

The sounds of beautiful, soft, sweet music.

What talent this hermit had!

"We must tell Hua about this wonderful music we have heard right away," said the chief officer.

But when they reached their leader, Hua began to laugh.

"A hermit playing the chin in the watchtower of a city that is going to be destroyed?" he asked. "What is the matter with all of you?

"I will go to see for myself."

And with that, Hua and his son climbed upon their horses and began to ride toward the open gates of Hsi Cheng.

When they got there, they saw just what the

scouts had seen. And when they looked up at the watchtower, they saw even more!

You see, Hua was also very clever. He knew right away that the hermit was Chuko.

But there were things Hua didn't understand. Why was this leader of the Shu army sitting, smiling, and singing on the wall of a city that was about to be destroyed?

One of the chin boys stood beside Chuko, resting his hand on the top of a jeweled sword. The other was gently waving a whip made from a white yak's tail.

Directly in front of the hermit, soft gray puffs of smoke were rising up into the sky from an incense burner.

Everything looked so peaceful and quiet.

Hua looked at the workers, who moved slowly. They continued to sweep the leaves from the city's streets.

There was no other sign of life.

Hua turned to face his soldiers, who were right behind him. He gave one order: "Retreat! Go back!"

The soldiers stared at their leader in surprise.

"But, Father!" shouted Hua's son. "Why? Why should we go back?"

"Hush, my son," said Hua. "You are still a young man. You do not understand what is going on. Chuko is a very clever general. The city gates were open. We must ask ourselves why. Maybe his soldiers are hiding. Or maybe he has some other trick that will trap us!"

The Wei soldiers looked at one another. Hua could be right! And they turned around and went back to their kingdom.

Now as soon as they were out of sight, Chuko handed the chin to the chin boys who carried it away.

Then he began to laugh!

Soon the city officials and the handful of soldiers in worker dress gathered around Chuko. People started to come out of their hiding places.

No one could quite understand what they had just seen. But everyone was so grateful that they knelt before this great leader.

"Your Excellency, please tell us what happened," said one of the city officials. "Hua, a great general, had a strong army behind him. Yet he ran away from an empty city. What does that mean?"

Chuko smiled.

"My dear friends, Hua could not understand why I would take a chance like this," Chuko said. "I think he thought we were going to trick him."

And with that, Chuko began to laugh again!

This Hound Hath Loved Me

🐞 🐞 🐞 🐞 🐞 🐞 🐞

The way we treat others will have an effect on our lives. As this story illustrates, jealousy and hatred will not fuel us for where we want to go in life. They leave our tanks empty. And we are stalled by the side of the road. But compassion and faithfulness will take us all the way on our journey to find true happiness.

Once upon a time many years ago in India, there was a big family of princes and cousins who just couldn't get along with one another.

They argued and disagreed about everything.

One evening King Pandav, the father of the five princes, lay dying. His blind brother, Kuru, sat beside him.

"I know I will not get well. And my five sons are still too young to carry on in my place," the King told him. "Will you please rule the land as long as you live? And see that my sons are trained as kings should be?"

Kuru agreed. And a few days later, he became the new ruler.

The blind King was honest and fair. And he remembered his promise to look after the young princes. Yudhisthir was the oldest. Bhima was second. And Arjun, the third. The youngest two were twins.

But at the same time the King forgot about his own sons. And they soon became mean and evil. Duryodhan was the oldest. Some say he was the one who talked his brothers into being so mean to their cousins.

One day Kuru announced that Yudhisthir, as the oldest, would be the next king to rule the land. His own sons became very angry. They did not want to be ruled by a Pandav prince.

A few weeks later in a faraway city, a big festival was being planned. Kuru was invited to go but was not feeling well. So he decided to send the Pandav princes and their mother instead. To honor their visit, a special house was built for the family.

What the Pandavs didn't know was that Duryodhan had ordered that every piece of wood used be soaked in oil.

That evening as the young princes and their mother slept, one of their cousins set fire to the house!

But luckily the family got out.

The builders had dug a tunnel underneath the house that led to the forest. So the brothers were able to carry their mother to safety.

The Pandavs knew that the Kurus had started the fire.

"Maybe if we stay in the forest, they will think we all died. Then our mother will be safe," said Yudhisthir.

The next day the brothers built a little house and joined a religious group called the Brahmans. Each day they would put on long brown robes and go out to beg for their bread, as the Brahmans did. And each night they would carry it home to their mother.

One day as they were out walking, the five Pandav brothers met some other Brahmans.

"Why don't you come along with us. We are on our way to Panchala for 'Bride's Choice,' " said one of the Brahmans.

" 'Bride's Choice'?" said Yudhisthir. "What is that?"

"Why, the man who is the best marksman with a bow and arrow will be permitted to marry the king's daughter," he answered.

Arjun's heart began to pound at the thought. This was because he knew he was a good marksman.

"We cannot go, my dear friends," said

Yudhisthir. "We are poor, and we have a mother to care for. So we must stay here."

"Why don't you bring your mother with you? We will travel slowly, begging as we go," said one of the Brahmans.

"There will be lots of good food for everyone once we get there. Besides, you are as handsome as princes. Maybe the princess will lose her heart to one of you."

The five brothers looked at one another and decided to join the band of Brahmans. The journey took them down many long, dusty roads. But finally they reached the city of Panchala where hundreds of people stood waiting.

It looked like everyone in India was there!

Nonetheless, they found a room in a little cottage, just outside the gates to the city. And each morning the five Pandav brothers left their mother to rest while they went out to beg for food.

At last came the day of "Bride's Choice." Kings and queens gathered under bright red canopies to see which young man would win the contest—and the hand of Princess Draupadi.

As they sat and watched, Draupadi appeared in a wedding gown. She carried a garland of colorful flowers that she planned to place around the neck of the winner.

Draupadi's brother, the Prince, walked her to

the altar where a priest stood ready and waiting to perform the wedding vows. Then the young prince held up his father's war bow for all to see.

"Behold the bow of Drupad, my father," the young Prince began. "By the ancient custom of our fathers, today we celebrate 'Bride's Choice.'

"Anyone born of Arya blood, be he rich or poor, may enter. Whoever can shoot five arrows from this bow through a whirling ring and hit the target may claim my sister, the Princess Draupadi, as his bride."

The crowd began to cheer.

"Behold, my sister, these monarchs and princes have come to seek your hand," the Prince said. "Here is the brave Duryodhan and his brothers of the house of Kuru. Here are Kalinga and Tamra from the eastern ocean. Here is Pattan who rules the western shore . . ."

And he continued to give the name and fame of each one.

One by one, the young men stepped forward to try their luck. And one by one, they walked away in defeat. Many did not have the strength even to bend the bow.

Not a single arrow reached the target.

"The test is impossible," said one young man. "All of us have been tricked. King Drupad has made us look silly in front of great queens and this crowd."

The five brothers stood with the Brahmans and did not say a word.

Finally young Arjun looked at Yudhisthir.

Yudhisthir nodded.

Arjun walked toward the bow.

The crowd grew quiet. Who was this young man? No one knew.

Arjun lifted the bow, took an arrow, then nodded to the beautiful Princess Draupadi, who was watching him.

Arjun drew back and released the bow.

The arrow hit the target!

So did the next one. And the next. Until all five arrows had met the mark.

Suddenly Princess Draupadi left her brother's side and walked toward young Arjun. She placed the flowers around his neck and stood beside him.

The crowd began to cheer once again.

The Brahmans screamed with delight.

But the young men who had tried so hard and lost were angry!

How could a young, ragged beggar boy be better than they were?

The young men began to run toward the King, the Prince, and Draupadi herself! How dare she turn her back on kings and warriors for a simple beggar, they shouted.

But the Pandav brothers were ready.

They ran from their place and formed a human wall around King Drupad and his children.

"Be calm and listen to me, my people," said the King. "This young man who you think is a beggar is one of you. I knew him the moment he drew back the bow. He is Arjun, son of Pandav. And these are his four brothers.

"I don't know why they came to our city dressed like beggars. But they are princes, not priests," the King continued. "I am proud to give my daughter to any son of the house of Pandav."

The Kuru princes looked at one another and moved away.

The Pandav brothers were so excited. They couldn't wait for their mother to meet Princess Draupadi.

"Mother! Mother! Come see this wonderful prize we brought home today," they shouted as they reached the humble cottage where she sat waiting.

"You do not have to share it with me, my sons," she began. "Share your prize with one another."

And then she saw Draupadi.

What did she say? Would her words cause her sons to quibble and quarrel with one another?

Yet the words of a mother cannot be taken back or disobeyed.

Arjun smiled.

It was he who had won the Princess, and he

loved her. But nothing must come between him and his brothers.

Besides, he would obey his mother's command.

"Yudhisthir is the oldest, and he is to be king," Arjun said. "I want him to marry Draupadi. And she can be queen to all of us.

"When the time comes for the rest of us to marry, each of us will choose a bride. But Draupadi will always be First Queen."

A few weeks later Yudhisthir and Draupadi were married. They lived a good life, became very rich, and were much loved by everyone.

But time marched on.

One day the five Pandav brothers and Draupadi decided to give the kingdom to their children. And they would travel across the desert to find the City of the Gods. There they would live out the rest of their lives.

Following close behind them was a dog— Yudhisthir's faithful hound.

The sands burned their feet every day, and the winds chilled them at night. Yet they knew they must travel on.

Yudhisthir felt sorry for the old hound and ordered it go back home. But the dog would not listen.

Day by day, the travelers grew weaker. And one by one, they passed on.

Finally only Yudhisthir was left—Yudhisthir and the hound.

One morning Yudhisthir awoke to a bright light. It was the Lord Indra.

"Climb aboard my chariot," he said. "I have come to take you the rest of the way to the City of the Gods. Your wife and brothers are waiting for you."

Yudhisthir started to climb into the chariot. Then he stopped and turned around.

"There is one more thing I must take with me, Lord," he said. "I cannot leave my hound behind."

Indra's face grew dark.

"You don't need that beast there," he said. "Why, he isn't even clean."

"I cannot leave him," Yudhisthir said. "This hound has eaten my food, shared my losses, and loved me."

The Lord Indra looked down at Yudhisthir from the golden chariot.

Suddenly the Lord smiled. "Climb in, my son," he said. "And do bring the hound with you.

"You see, you have passed the last test. You have lived a good life. You have been kind to everyone. Even a poor, ugly, dirty dog—a beautiful friend who loved you."

Yudhisthir and the hound boarded the chariot. And Lord Indra drove them off to eternity.

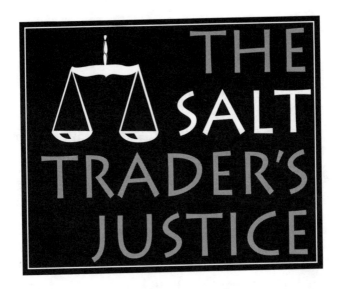

THE SALT TRADER'S JUSTICE

How would you feel if you were being honest, but you were surrounded by people trying to lie and cheat? How would you make people see that you were truthful? This story shows that in the end, people usually get what they deserve.

Once upon a time in a country called Egypt, there lived a kind and humble man.

He was a salt trader—a *Sekhti*.

The Sekhti was a poor peasant. He worked very hard each day to earn a living.

Every morning he would get up very early, go to the small stable in his yard, and share his breakfast with his donkey.

Then he would hang two big baskets of salt on either side of the animal. And the two would be on their way.

Trading salt was not an easy way to make a living.

The Sekhti had to drive his donkey many miles to reach the market. There he could trade his salt for milk, meat, or bread. But by working long hours every day, the Sekhti was able to bring home enough food to take care of his family.

And that was all that really mattered.

The Sekhti never got tired of traveling the same roads. One of them took him along a narrow path. It ran between a canal and a wheat field on land owned by a rich man.

Now the land was being taken care of by a servant named Tehuti-nekht. He was the type who tried to make everyone in the whole Nile Valley think he was more important than he really was.

Each day he watched the Sekhti drive his donkey down the long narrow path to the market.

It should not have bothered him. But it did.

"Every morning he comes along here with that old donkey," said Tehuti-nekht. "What's more, he hasn't given me anything for using *my* road."

Of course, it wasn't his road at all. But Tehuti-nekht was puffed up about his job as caretaker.

One morning the Sekhti was talking happily

to his donkey as they walked along. Just before they got to the narrow path, Tehuti-nekht appeared and threw his coat down in front of them. One end was in the water of the canal. The other end was in the wheat field.

The Sekhti stopped his donkey and looked at the coat.

He had to get to the market, so he had to keep walking.

"Wait just a minute, my dear man," said Tehuti-nekht. "You're not really going to walk that beast over my coat, are you?"

The poor peasant looked at Tehuti-nekht. Although he had never seen him before, Tehuti-nekht looked like a very important man.

"I'll try my best, sir, to go around," the Sekhti answered. And he turned the donkey toward the wheat field.

"What? You plan to have that beast stomp through my wheat instead?" shouted Tehuti-nekht.

"But the coat, sir, is blocking the path," said the Sekhti. "If I cannot drive my donkey over the coat, and I cannot take him around it, I will have to turn around and go back home. That is, unless you decide to pick up the coat."

Tehuti-nekht puffed up his shoulders and pursed his lips. His eyes grew dark and mean.

"How dare you say something like that to me,

you . . . you . . . donkey driver," sputtered Tehuti-nekht. "The coat will stay there until I decide to pick it up."

Well, there are times when we can't control those things that happen around us. This was one of those times.

While the Sekhti and Tehuti-nekht were talking, the donkey grew tired of waiting. So he decided to eat some of the sweet-smelling green wheat!

Just as he snapped off the first mouthful, Tehuti-nekht turned around and saw him.

"Thief! Thief! That donkey is a thief!" shouted Tehuti-nekht. "That's the last straw! You, my servants, come here and take this donkey away from the Sekhti."

The salt trader looked up in surprise.

"I'm so sorry, your lordship," he began. "I will pay for the wheat he ate if you will only let him go."

But Tehuti-nekht would not listen to the Sekhti. And he ordered his servants to throw the Sekhti into the canal.

The poor Sekhti.

His clothes had been torn. He was all muddy. And now Tehuti-nekht had his donkey!

"You have no right to abuse me like this," said the Sekhti as he started to get up. "I am only a poor salt trader. But I will seek justice."

Tehuti-nekht turned and glared at the peasant. Then he ordered the servants to push him back in the muddy water again.

"You can't talk that way to me," laughed Tehuti-nekht as he walked away.

Now the owner of the land where all this happened was Lord Steward Meruit, an important judge at the court of Pharaoh. The Sekhti had heard about the judge. But he was unaware that Meruit was the owner of the disputed land.

The Sekhti had been told that the judge was very fair to those who had been mistreated. This gave him a little hope. He decided to go to Meruit's court and tell the judge what had happened. He hoped the judge would make Tehuti-nekht return the donkey.

It seemed like a simple thing to do. Surely the judge would rule in his favor, thought the Sekhti.

But when he got to Meruit's court, there were hundreds of people in the halls, on the stairs, and in the street. They all wanted to see the judge too.

Everyone had a long list of wrongs that needed to be righted.

Can things in Egypt be this bad? thought the Sekhti.

But they were worse! As the Sekhti began to talk with some of the complainers, he soon discovered that many of them were lying.

Little lies. Middle-sized lies. And total whoppers!

The poor salt trader was very sad.

"If everyone stands in court and lies, how will an honest man ever be believed?" he asked himself, over and over again. He hoped Meruit would be a wise judge.

But in those days in Egypt, anyone who felt he had been treated unfairly was not able to speak to the judge right away. First he had to speak to advisors and courtiers, people who worked for the court.

Some of them didn't seem interested in the Sekhti's story. But he kept repeating it.

He wanted justice. He needed his donkey to earn a living. And he believed that the judge would be kind and fair.

Finally the salt trader got his day in court.

He held up his head and spoke loud and clear. He told the judge about the caretaker of the land and the coat on the path.

"He took my donkey, and now I have no way to make a living and feed my family," said the salt trader.

Meruit looked, listened, and said nothing. Finally he turned to one of his advisers. "Please ask the Sekhti to return tomorrow," the judge said.

That evening Meruit went to the Pharaoh.

"A Sekhti was in my court today. And I don't know what to do about his case," Meruit began. "You see, he complained against one of my very own servants. Now normally, this would make me very angry. But the Sekhti spoke very well for himself.

"My problem is this. There are so many people who tell me lies. I can't decide if this poor salt trader is lying or not."

The Pharaoh listened to Meruit's story. He then took a sip of his tea before speaking.

"You must test him then," the Pharaoh said. "But in the meantime make sure that his family is taken care of while he is unable to make a living."

So Meruit ordered his advisers to take food to the Sekhti's family while he was away from home.

"Just make sure that they don't know who is sending it," he said.

The next day when the Sekhti returned to court, Meruit's guards chased him away, telling him he was lying.

The Sekhti was confused. He knew he was not lying. So he returned the following day, pouring out his protest to the judge.

And once again, the guards chased him out of the courtroom.

And so it happened a third and a fourth time.

Still the Sekhti believed that he had been

mistreated by Tehuti-nekht. And he had a good reason to be there.

"Even if a man is powerful and great, he should not be allowed to rob the poor," the salt trader said. "I will go tomorrow and the day after that. And I will continue to go until justice has won."

And so he did.

But each time the guards chased him away.

Finally on the ninth day, the Sekhti decided to go to court one last time.

"I guess if I get chased away again, I will have to find some other way to make a living and care for my family," the Sekhti said.

But he had no idea what he would do.

That morning when the Sekhti entered the courtroom, Meruit looked down at the poor salt trader and smiled at him.

Finally Meruit had been convinced.

"A liar would not have so much determination," he said.

And with that, Meruit ruled that his own servant, Tehuti-nekht, the caretaker of his land, be stripped of his title, position, and power.

"You, my dear Sekhti, have proved to be honest and fair," said Meruit. "I know you are a good salt trader. But I wonder if you would like to come to work for me."

The Sekhti smiled. He had not expected this

honor. What would his wife and family say? He could not wait to tell them!

"Yes! Yes! I would be most honored to be your humble servant," the Sekhti answered.

"Then so it will be," smiled Meruit.

A few days later the Sekhti moved his family to the big house on Meruit's land. There he continued to be kind, fair, and honest with others.

Soon the Sekhti was known as one of the most honest men in Egypt. And in time, he became adviser to the Pharaoh himself.

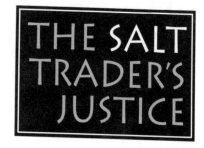

THE PLAY

Cast of Characters

Narrator

Tehuti-nekht

Old man

Sekhti

Meruit

Pharaoh

ACT ONE

Narrator: Many years ago in a small village in Egypt, there lived a poor peasant who was a salt trader. He was known as a *Sekhti*. Each morning he would get up very early, go to the small stable on his property, and share his breakfast with his donkey. After they finished, he would hang a big basket of salt on either side of the animal. And the two would begin their long walk to the market. Trading salt for meat, milk, or bread was not an easy way to make a living. But the Sekhti worked long hours every day so he could bring home enough food to take care of his family.

Sekhti: Well, are you ready to go again, my friend? We have a long way to go today.

Narrator: Of course, animals don't talk, as you know. So the donkey never answered him. But the Sekhti felt better just being able to talk with someone. Besides, there was no one else around to talk to. Until one morning when he came to the narrow path which ran between a canal and a wheat field. In his daily travels he had never noticed the man who stood there that morning. He looked very important.

Sekhti: What is this on the ground?

Tehuti-nekht: Why, what do you think it is? It's my cloak, donkey driver.

Narrator: Now, Tehuti-nekht was the caretaker of the land between the canal and the wheat field. He was a mean man. And he had decided that he didn't want the poor peasant walking past the property. That's why he decided to throw his cloak on the ground.

Sekhti: Please, sir, I'm on my way to the market to trade some salt. So would you please pick up your cloak so I may pass by?

Tehuti-nekht: Pick up my coat? Of course not! How dare you ask me a question like that!

Sekhti: Well, then, I guess we can go around.

Tehuti-nekht: Go around? You mean you're going let that beast stamp on my wheat?

Sekhti: Well, sir, if I cannot drive my donkey over the coat and cannot take him around it, I will have to go back home. There is no other way to get to the market.

Tehuti-nekht: So, go then, and see if I care!

Narrator: Well, sometimes things just happen that we aren't able to control. This was one of those times. While the Sekhti and Tehuti-nekht were talking, the donkey got tired of waiting. And he decided to take a bite of the wheat. But as soon as he heard the snap, Tehuti-nekht turned around quickly and saw him.

Tehuti-nekht: Thief! Thief! That donkey is a thief! Come here, my servants, and take that donkey away from the salt trader.

Sekhti: Oh, please, sir! He didn't mean to steal anything from you. After all, he's just an animal. I will pay you for what he ate, but please let him go.

Tehuti-nekht: Pay you will! You, servant, grab that man and throw him into the canal.

Narrator: The servants did as they were told. They pushed the salt trader into the muddy water.

As they did so, they tore his jacket. But even worse, Tehuti-nekht had his donkey.

Sekhti: You have no right to treat me like this. I am only a poor salt trader. I want you to know that I will seek justice.

Tehuti-nekht: How dare you talk to me that way? Don't you know that I am a very important man? Servants, throw him back into the water again.

Narrator: The servants did as they were told once again, while Tehuti-nekht walked away laughing.

ACT TWO

Narrator: The next morning, the Sekhti got up very early and decided to walk to town. He had heard that there was a judge at the court of Pharaoh who was very kind and fair to those who had been mistreated. He decided to go to the city to visit him.

Sekhti: I just know if I can go to the court of Lord Steward Meruit and tell him what happened, he will make Tehuti-nekht give me my donkey back.

Narrator: But when the salt trader got to the city, there were hundreds of people everywhere—

in the halls, on the stairs, and in the street. Everyone wanted to see the judge too. Everyone had a long list of wrongs that needed to be righted.

Sekhti: Oh, my! Are things in Egypt really this bad, old man?

Old Man: I'm afraid so, salt trader. I understand that it takes a lot of time for Meruit to make a decision because so many people lie to him.

Sekhti: *Lie* to him? But that is not right!

Old Man: Right or wrong, they are doing it. Little lies, middle-sized lies, and total whoppers.

Sekhti: And what about those of us who tell the truth? Will he believe us?

Old Man: All you can do is stand in line and wait your turn, salt trader. And just see what happens.

Narrator: Now in those days in Egypt, people who felt they had been mistreated had to speak to court people before they got their chance to speak to the judge. No problem. The Sekhti told his story. Unfortunately, he had to tell it over and over again. He wanted justice. He needed his donkey to make a living. And Tehuti-nekht had taken it from him. Finally after talking to many court people, he was told the judge would see him.

Sekhti: Good morning, sir.

Meruit: Good morning, salt trader. And what is your problem today?

Sekhti: I am very sad because an evil man took my donkey. And now I have no way to make a living and feed my family.

Meruit: What happened—and who was this man?

Sekhti: Well, every day I walk my donkey from my house to the market to sell my salt. One morning I came to the path between the canal and the wheat field, right outside the entrance to the market. And a man named Tehuti-nekht threw down his cloak and would not let me pass. When I tried to go around, he told me I could not drive my donkey through his wheat field.

Meruit: Yes, go on.

Sekhti: While we were talking, my donkey took a bite of his wheat. So he ordered his servants to take my donkey from me and push me into the canal.

Narrator: Meruit turned pale. He looked down at the poor peasant but said nothing. Finally he turned to one of his advisers and asked him to tell the Sekhti to come back the following day.

ACT THREE

Narrator: That evening the judge went to the Pharaoh's home for dinner. He knew he had to talk to someone who was very wise and could help him solve this problem. He began his story after dinner as they were sipping their tea.

Meruit: A Sekhti was in my court today, dear Pharaoh, and I don't know what to do. You see, he complained against one of my very own servants.

Pharaoh: Yes, and did that make you angry?

Meruit: Well, usually it would, but the Sekhti seemed so honest when he talked to me.

Pharaoh: Then what is the problem?

Meruit: Well, there are so many people who lie to me every day. I can't decide if this poor salt trader is lying or not.

Pharaoh: Then you must test him. See how many times he will come back to seek justice.

Meruit: That is a good idea, Pharaoh. I will do that.

Pharaoh: But in the meantime, make sure that his family is taken care of. Send them food. But don't let them know who it's from.

Narrator: So the next day when the Sekhti returned to court, Meruit's guards chased him away, telling him he was lying. The Sekhti was confused. Why would the judge think that? It was the truth. Maybe he needed to hear the story once again. So the Sekhti went back again the next day. And the same thing happened. Once again the guards chased him out of the courtroom. And so it happened six, seven, eight times.

Sekhti: I have been there eight times, and I can't understand why the judge won't believe me. Even if a man is powerful and great, he should not be allowed to rob the poor.

Narrator: After eight attempts the Sekhti decided he would go to the courtroom one last time. He needed to get home to take care of his family. The next morning the Sekhti arrived bright and early.

Meruit: Aha, so you have returned one more time, salt trader.

Sekhti: Yes, judge. One more time. I am confused. I have told many court people and you the truth. And I don't understand why no one believes me. I am not a man who tells lies.

Narrator: The wise judge looked down at the salt trader. His mind was made up.

Sekhti: Are you going to have your guards chase me away again? It won't be necessary. I will go quietly. I cannot wait for justice any longer. I must go home and care for my family.

Meruit: No, dear salt trader, I will not have anyone chase you away today. I know now you are telling the truth. A liar would not have so much determination.

Sekhti: Oh, thank you, sir. Thank you for believing in me, because I did not lie.

Meruit: Now, one more thing. How would you like to come to work for me?

Sekhti: Work for you, sir?

Meruit: Yes, you see I need a new caretaker for my land. Tehuti-nekht no longer works for me. And I also need someone to care for your donkey!

Narrator: The Sekhti looked at the judge in surprise. He did not know that Meruit owned that land.

Sekhti: Yes! Yes! I would be most honored.

Meruit: Then it shall be so. Now hurry on home and get your family together.

Narrator: The Sekhti ran out the door. He could not wait to tell his wife. And he could not wait to see his donkey, who was truly a friend. A few days later the Sekhti moved his family to the big house on Meruit's land. He tried not to puff himself up as Tehuti-nekht had done. He remained kind, fair, and honest. And in a few years the Sekhti was rewarded again. He became the adviser to the Pharaoh himself.